Blob

Frieda Wishinsky

Orca currents

ORCA BOOK PUBLISHERS

Library and Archives Canada Cataloguing in Publication

Wishinsky, Frieda

Blob / written by Frieda Wishinsky.

(Orca currents)

ISBN 978-1-55469-182-1 (bound).--ISBN 978-1-55469-181-4 (pbk.)

I. Title. II. Series: Orca currents

PS8595.I834B56 2010   jC813'.54   C2009-906831-1

First published in the United States, 2010
Library of Congress Control Number: 2009940776

Summary: Eve is overweight, and her self-image is suffering until she
joins a mentoring program and learns to accept herself the way she is.

Orca Book Publishers gratefully acknowledges the support for its publishing
programs provided by the following agencies: the Government of Canada
through the Canada Book Fund and the Canada Council for the Arts, and
the Province of British Columbia
through the BC Arts Council and the Book Publishing Tax Credit.

Cover design by Teresa Bubela
Cover photography by Getty Images

Orca Book Publishers
PO Box 5626, Station B
Victoria, BC Canada
V8R 6S4

Orca Book Publishers
PO Box 468
Custer, WA USA
98240-0468

www.orcabook.com
Printed and bound in Canada.
Printed on 100% PCW recycled paper.
13 12 11 10 • 4 3 2 1

"I never forget a face, but in your case I'll be glad to make an exception."

—Groucho Marks

chapter one

It's the first day of school and my heart is pounding. It always pounds on the first day, but this year is worse. We moved to a new neighborhood this summer, and I'm starting high school. I know almost no one at South View High—except Sarah.

I'm glad she'll be there. I've known her since grade three. She was away in California this summer, but we spoke on the phone last week. She's as nervous about high school as I am.

I hurry toward the red brick building. *Phew!* Sarah is standing on the top step talking to Zoe Campbell. I didn't know Zoe was going to South View. Zoe towers over Sarah. Zoe used to be short. I can't believe how much she grew over the summer.

I'm almost at the bottom step. I'm about to call out to Sarah and tell her to wait up. Before I can say a word, I hear Zoe. "Are you still friends with Eve?" Her words blast out.

What? I stop walking. Why is Zoe talking about me? Why is she talking so loudly that all the kids rushing into school can hear?

Sarah nods.

"I saw Eve on the street this summer," says Zoe. "She's gotten *so* fat. She looks like a blob."

I feel like a herd of horses are stomping through my chest. I want to turn and run, but my feet are glued to the pavement.

"She's just a little overweight," says Sarah.

"Have you seen her gut? It jiggles like jelly. She must have hit on every candy bar in the city. I'd be embarrassed to be seen with her." Zoe tosses her long brown hair.

"I'm not embarrassed." Sarah's voice is shaky and uncertain.

I want to shout, *Sarah! This is me you're talking about. Me! Eve! Your friend. Tell Zoe I'm not a blob. Tell her I'm your friend, and you don't care what she says.*

But Sarah says nothing. Kids pass me up the stairs and into the building.

I watch Sarah and Zoe walk into school as the bell rings.

Blob! The word hammers through my head. *Blob. Blob. Blob.*

I know I've gained weight this summer. Almost none of my clothes fit me anymore. I'm wearing a pair of jeans that were loose last year. Now I can barely zip them up. And I can't button the top button. I've used a safety pin instead.

My dad's big shirts cover my bulging middle, but he's complaining that he has nothing to wear. I've been taking all his good shirts.

It was that dumb job at the convenience store. Every time the owner barked at me, I ate. She barked all the time, so I ate all the time. I ate cookies, pretzels, potato chips and ice cream. A double chocolate cone always cheers me up.

Now I'm fat and I'm going to be the butt of Zoe's jokes. Why does she have to go to this school? Why is she being snarky about me? What did I ever do to her?

And what's with Sarah? It looks like I can't count on her to stand up for me.

Why did I let myself snack all summer? If I hadn't, I wouldn't look like this. Then Zoe couldn't call me a blob.

The bell rings again. I know I have to go in, but I can't move. If I don't run, I'm going to be late. Then everyone will stare at me when I walk into class.

I force my feet to move. I dash into the building. Now I'm sweating. My armpits are getting so damp little ponds are forming. I race down the hall and sweat drips from my face. I dab at it with a crumpled tissue. I hope I don't smell as sweaty as I feel.

I fly into room eight, my new homeroom.

I spy Sarah sitting in the third row, and I slide in beside her. She gives me a half smile. I take a deep breath. Calm down, I tell myself. She's still your friend.

That's when I see the note. Sarah tries to shove it into her English book, but I read it before she hides it. It's written in big black letters.

No one wants to hang around with a Blob, Sarah. Trust me. See you later.

"A true friend is someone who thinks that you are a good egg even though he knows that you are slightly cracked."

—Bernard Meltzer

chapter two

I know Zoe wrote the note. Zoe and I never hung around together in middle school, but we weren't enemies—at least not till today. Why is she treating me like this?

"Hi, Sarah," I mutter.

"Hi, Eve," Sarah answers, but she doesn't look up from her book. I know she wonders if I read the note.

Our homeroom teacher, Ms. Roberts, talks about rules, schedules and clubs, but all I can think about is that note in Sarah's book. All I can hear is the word *blob* ringing in my ear.

I remember Annie Lucas in middle school. Annie was tall and fat. Kids called her Porky, Blubber, Beach Ball, Elephant Girl. They came up with a new nasty name every day. Annie never said a word. She hardly spoke to anyone. She sat alone at lunch, munching the same sandwich day after day—egg salad with gobs of mayonnaise. I used to feel sorry for her, but I never tried to be her friend. I never said anything more than hello to her. I wasn't mean or anything, but I ignored her.

Sarah pokes me in the side. I look up.

"Eve Richards, are you here?" asks Ms. Roberts.

"Yes," I answer.

"I've called your name twice already. Please pay attention."

"Sorry," I mutter.

I see Zoe roll her eyes at Sarah. She mouths the words "stupid blob." A blond girl sitting beside Zoe laughs. Zoe puffs her cheeks and laughs too.

"What's going on?" Ms. Roberts snaps at Zoe.

"Nothing," says Zoe with a straight face.

"Then let's continue," says Ms. Roberts.

When the bell rings, I check my schedule. I have English with Mr. London after homeroom. "What's your first class?" I ask Sarah.

"Math." Sarah sticks her schedule into her backpack and stands up. "See you."

"Great. See you at lunch."

"I don't know if we have the same lunch hour," she says.

"When's yours?" I ask.

"Twelve."

"Mine too."

"Oh," says Sarah. "I guess I'll see you then. I'd better hurry. Math is on the second floor."

Sarah gives me a half wave and hurries out of the room. Zoe and the blond girl walk out too. I hear Zoe call, "Hey, Sarah. Wait up."

Why does Sarah want to be friends with Zoe? Why is Sarah unfriendly to me? I'm still the same person I was last year. Why is everything different now? Is it because I gained weight?

Thoughts whip around my head like a cyclone.

I want to stop thinking about this, but I can't. I don't want to go to my next class. I want to go home.

I take a deep breath. I tell myself I don't care that Sarah doesn't want to be friends. If that's the way she's going to act, she's not worth it. But no matter what I tell myself, I still feel like I've been socked in the stomach.

I pick up my backpack and head for room twelve. I walk slowly. Each step feels like a mile.

I can barely swallow. My saliva tastes like sour milk. I rummage in my backpack for a mint. I pop it into my mouth, but it doesn't help. Oh great! Now I probably have bad breath too! I am fat and sweaty, and I have bad breath. I'm a mess.

What if I'm Annie Lucas this year? What if I sit alone at lunch every day? What if I have no one to talk to, and Zoe keeps calling me names?

No! No! I can't be Annie Lucas. I have to do something.

I imagine punching Zoe in the face and knocking her teeth out. A toothless Zoe would have trouble calling me names. I smile at the thought. I know I could never do that, even if she deserves it. I've never hit anyone, except Robbie Peters in kindergarten. He had stomped on my toe to grab a racing car before I did. I had to sit in the time-out seat for half an hour for that. What can I do about Zoe? Maybe I could call her a snake. Match her nasty name for nasty name. She's as skinny as a snake and just as poisonous. But snake doesn't sound that bad. I have to think of a nastier name.

I feel a sharp jab in my shoulder. I hear someone yell, "Ouch!"

I look up.

I've collided with a boy. "Watch where you're going, stupid," he snarls.

"Sorry," I say.

He growls and walks away.

It's only 10:00 AM, and I hate school already.

"If you let a bully intimidate you,
he's going to do it again."

—**Charles Djou**

chapter three

Mr. London talks about the books we'll
be reading, the essays we'll be writing
and the exams we'll be taking. Why
does school always start with lists and
schedules?

Luckily in the last five minutes of class,
Mr. London gives me another idea. He tells
us about how he volunteered in a literacy
program in Africa this summer. He visited
an animal preserve and saw lions, tigers
and gerenuks, which are a kind of gazelle.

He says it's amazing how tall gerenuks are when you view them up close. He showed us a picture of one and it's a skinny, weird-looking animal.

Gerenuk! That's what I'll call Zoe. She probably has no idea what a gerenuk is. It sounds like something ugly though, and if I say it in just the right insulting voice it might work.

I'll fire off my insult as soon as Zoe hits me with *blob*. I have to stand up to Zoe or she'll never stop. Annie Lucas never stood up to anyone, and the kids pounded her with insults day after day. I can't let that happen to me.

I feel better as I head off to art class. Ms. Holmes, my art teacher, only spends ten minutes talking about schedules and rules. We start a project right away. We have to design ads for our favorite food. Favorite food? Easy! Chocolate, of course. I come up with this:

WANT TO GO TO HEAVEN AND STILL STAY ON EARTH?
EAT CHOCOLATE.

Ms. Holmes says it's original, fun and to the point. I feel great.

I draw a giant chocolate bar with angel wings. The bar is sailing through the air toward the open hand of a girl. She's looking longingly up at it. She can't wait to grab it. Eat it. Enjoy it.

The bar looks so delicious I want to eat it. I wish I had chocolate with my lunch. But I'd be nuts to eat chocolate. It will only make me blobbier. No matter how much I love chocolate, I have to resist it. It's healthy food from now till all my fat is gone.

The bell rings. Kids fly out of classrooms. I walk alone down the crowded hall toward the lunchroom. All I can think about is Zoe and Sarah. What if Zoe has the same lunch hour as us? What if she makes another crack about me in front of everyone? What if Sarah ignores me?

I tell myself it's just lunch. It's not the dentist or jail. But my stomach feels like marbles are banging around inside it. My mouth feels as dry as if I jammed a box of stale crackers into it.

Halfway down the hall, I hear Zoe behind me. I catch a few words. "Mia, did you see how she...," she says. "She's so..." Then she laughs.

I know she's talking about me. I know she wants me to hear. I want to turn around and scream at her. I want to tell her to shut up. I want to call her a gerenuk, but I can't.

I hurry into the lunchroom. Sarah is sitting at a table alone. I walk over to her.

"Hi, Sarah."

Sarah looks up from her yogurt. "Oh, hi."

"So how was your morning?" I sit beside her on the bench.

"Fine." Sarah's eyes dart around the room. I glance around and see that Zoe is heading toward us.

I clench my teeth. I will not move.

"Hi, Sarah," she says. "Oh, hi, Eve." She eyes my lunch bag. "What do you have in there? I hope it's not fattening."

Sarcasm drips like grease from her mouth. I want to smack her.

I try to think of something clever to lob back at her, but nothing comes to me. I just sit there. I don't know what to do so I pull a cheese sandwich out of my lunch bag.

"Is that low-fat cheese, Eve? I hope it is—for your sake," says Zoe.

"No. Regular cheese," I blurt out. My words sound lame, but I can't think of anything else to say. I bite into my sandwich.

Zoe makes a *tsk-tsk* sound with her tongue and wags her finger in my face. "You should really be careful what you put into your mouth, Eve. Well, I'd better go. Mia is waiting for me. She knows everybody at South View."

Zoe points to the blond girl who had been sitting beside her in homeroom. "Meet us later, Sarah," she says.

Sarah nods.

I watch Zoe walk away. Then Sarah stands up.

"I have to go too," she says. "I promised to help Libby Brown with homework."

Sarah hurries out of the lunchroom.

I'm the only one in the lunchroom eating by myself. I take another bite of sandwich.

The food sticks in my throat. I have to get out of here.

I pack up the rest of my food. I scoot out of the lunchroom and down the hall to the bathroom.

No one's there. It's quiet. It smells of bathroom cleaner but that's all.

I walk into a stall, sit down on the cold black and white tiles and eat my sandwich.

"You can't lose weight by talking about it.
You have to keep your mouth shut."

—Author Unknown

chapter four

A nasty smell fills the air. I have to get out of the bathroom or I'm going to gag. I dash out and wash my hands before the girl who made the smell comes out of her stall.

Eating lunch in the bathroom is gross. I can't do that again, but where else can I go? I don't want to eat alone in the lunchroom again.

When the bell rings at the end of the day, I grab my backpack and fly out the door. A block from school, I slow down. My head is spinning. All I can think about is Zoe and Sarah.

When I walk into the kitchen at home, Mom is slicing onions. "How was school?" she asks.

I know she wants me to say terrific, but I can't. It was not terrific. It was miserable.

"Fine," I mumble.

"Do you know any of the kids?"

"A few."

"Terrific," says Mom. Then she putters around the kitchen. I'm relieved she's too busy to drill me.

"I'm going to do my homework," I tell her.

"I'll call you when supper is ready. Dad's working late."

I head for my room and sprawl on my bed. I only have a little homework—a short essay on great scientific discoveries of the twentieth century.

I close my eyes. I read that if you need to clear your head you should close your eyes, take deep breaths and think of nothing. Thinking of nothing works for a minute and a half. Then Zoe's sneering face looms up. I can almost hear her cackle "Blob" at me like a witch. I try to blink her face away. I try to shake her voice out of my head.

I turn on my computer and google *scientific discoveries twentieth century* and hit the first entry. It's nothing useful. I hit the second and third. There's not much I can use there either. I glance at the top of the screen. There are two million entries for scientific discoveries! There are robots, comets, telescopes and cures for nasty diseases like scurvy.

I start to read entry number four on discoveries in astronomy, but my mind wanders back to Sarah and Zoe. "I will not let them get to me," I say out loud. But I need a plan.

I type in the word *diet*. There are over forty-three million entries for diets! That's forty-one million more entries for diets than there are for scientific discoveries.

There are millions of ways to lose weight.
I start randomly clicking on links.

There's the lemonade diet and the
chicken soup diet. I consider those, but
lemonade makes my teeth hurt, and chicken
soup is too hot for early September. I nix
the lazybones diet, the cabbage soup diet
and the blueberry diet. The One Good Meal
diet sounds like something you do before
you are executed.

I check out a page with diet tips. I like tip
number one about chewing gum whenever
you feel hungry. I can't do that in school,
but maybe I can skip breakfast and chew
gum instead. But tip number two says to
never skip breakfast. Tip number three says
to take one day at a time. I can do that. All
I need is the right diet.

I spot the You Can Do It in Seven Days
diet. On Monday you're allowed to eat all
the fruit you want except bananas. A whole
day of fruit? I like fruit but...

On day two you can eat all the vegetables
you want. You can even add mustard,

soy sauce or vinegar. I like most vegetables but a whole day of them? And adding mustard, soy sauce or vinegar to them doesn't sound any tastier.

Day three is much better. All the fruit and vegetables you want. But day four is weird—five bananas and five glasses of milk. I hate milk except chocolate milk. I would barf on day four. But maybe barfing is part of the diet. Maybe it helps you lose weight. I don't have to become bulimic or anything. I could just have one barfy day a week. Then again, maybe I'll grow to love bananas and milk.

I'll give the You Can Do It in Seven Days diet a try.

"Probably nothing in the world arouses more false hope than the first hours of a diet."

—Dan Bennett

chapter five

When I wake up on day one of my diet, I'm almost excited. I shoot out of bed and head down for breakfast. I gobble down a pear and an apple. I pack another apple and a pear and some grapes into a baggie for lunch.

"All I want for supper is fruit," I tell Mom, "so don't worry about cooking for me. I'm on a diet."

"All you eat on this diet is fruit? That's crazy," says Mom. "You'll get sick."

"No the first day is just fruit. Tomorrow I can eat vegetables. But just vegetables."

Before Mom has time to lecture me about my crazy diet, I'm out the door.

I decide to smile no matter what happens today. After all, today is a new beginning. Today is the first day of my diet. Today I will not let Zoe or Sarah get to me.

A block from school, I see Carolyn and Denise heading toward South View. I went to middle school with them. I know them well enough to say hi, so I catch up with them.

"Hi!" I say.

They both smile and return the greeting.

"I like your hair short," I tell Carolyn.

Carolyn beams as she runs her hand through her red curls. "Thanks. I thought it would look horrible this short, but now I love it. How was your first day?"

"Fine," I say, smiling. I'm relieved I know someone at South View besides Sarah and Zoe. "How about you?"

"I hate math already. I don't understand a word Ms. Murray says. She thinks everyone is a math genius. Well, I'm not. I love Ms. Holmes in art though."

"Me too," I say.

"Are you joining any clubs?" asks Denise.

"I haven't thought about it," I say. "What are you joining?"

"Choir for sure. So are Zoe and Sarah from middle school," says Denise.

"Oh," I say. "I can't sing."

"Well, there are lots of other clubs. Did you see the list?"

"Not yet. I think I stuffed it into my backpack. It must be in there somewhere."

"If you have a twelve o'clock lunch, I'll show you my list in case you lost yours," Denise offers.

"Thanks. That would be great." I try to sound matter-of-fact. I don't want them to know how happy I am to have someone to eat lunch with.

In homeroom I smile at Sarah as I slide into my seat. She gives me another one of her half smiles. This one is actually more like a quarter of a smile. Her lips barely turn up. Sarah's smiles are getting skinnier by the day.

After roll call Ms. Roberts reminds us to sign up for clubs by Friday. I peek into my backpack. I see a wad of papers and, yes, there's the list of clubs. I pull it out. Photography? Maybe. Knitting? No. Running Club? No. Volleyball? Maybe.

The bell rings. Sarah mutters a "See ya" and scuttles off. I gather up my stuff and head for the next class, music appreciation.

The room is packed. There's only one seat left in the back. I hurry toward it. It's right beside Zoe.

"You're in this class too?" she says. She inches her chair away from me. I try to ignore her. I glue my eyes to the front of the room. Zoe keeps moving her chair farther and farther away from me as if I had bad breath. Mr. Munroe asks us to sing in rounds as an icebreaker. I can't sing in key, so I sing as low as I can.

"Don't sing," hisses Zoe just loud enough that the kids in our row can hear. A couple of kids snicker when Zoe clutches her chest like she's been stabbed in the heart.

"You should never sing. You have an awful voice. I thought fat people were good singers. So many opera singers are fat."

I want to slap her. I want to call her names much worse than snake or gerenuk. I bite my tongue to stop the tears from welling up. I will not let Zoe or anyone see how I feel. I try so hard not to cry I cannot hear a sound in the room.

How dare Zoe make me feel like this? I take a deep breath. I force myself to listen to Mr. Munroe. He's talking about how to hit high and low notes. I just want to hit Zoe.

When the bell rings, I dash down the hall and into the bathroom. No one is there. I walk into a stall, yank off a handful of toilet paper and sob.

I hear someone coming in. I muffle my tears, wipe my eyes with more toilet paper and flush it down.

By lunch I'm calmer. I shove Zoe to the back of my mind. I laugh with Denise and Carolyn. I joke about my fruit lunch and my crazy diet. I tell them my diet plan for

the week. They can't believe I can stick to it.
I assure them I will. I look longingly at their
sandwiches. I want cheese. I want bread.
I want eggs, chicken and chocolate. I want
real food, not seven-day-diet food.

How can I eat vegetables all day tomorrow? I'm already sick of fruit after only half
a day.

"Bigger snacks mean bigger slacks."

—**Author Unknown**

chapter six

"I bought lots of fruit and vegetables for you," Mom says when I get home from school.

The fruit bowl is a pyramid of pears, peaches, bananas and plums. Two cantaloupes are ripening on the counter beside a basket of tomatoes.

I open the fridge. It's bursting with apples, grapes, carrots, broccoli, string beans, lettuce, cucumbers, radishes and zucchini. How can I eat all this stuff?

I know Mom is trying to be helpful. She didn't say anything about my weight all summer, but I caught her eyeing me up and down a few times. It was like she was mentally weighing me. I could almost hear her think, *How many pounds has Eve gained today? How can I make her stop eating? Should I hide the food? Should I only buy sprouts?*

I don't want to have to talk to my mom about my diet, so I head to my room. There's a magazine on my bed. It's open to an article about the increase in obesity and diabetes in teenagers. I walk into the bathroom. The magazine in the wicker basket is opened to an article on weight gain and self-image. Beside it is a book called *Just Do It*. I read the back cover of the book. The book is about changing habits. It says you can change a habit in six easy steps. And the first habit is food addiction.

I don't want to read articles about being fat! I'm not a food addict! At least I wasn't till I started dieting. Now all I can think about is food. And these articles just make me think about food more.

I charge out of my room and into the kitchen. "Mom, don't leave me any more articles about food!" I snap. "It makes me crazy. I'm trying to diet and it's hard enough. I hate being fat. I hate dieting, and your articles are making everything worse."

"I'm sorry, Eve," says Mom. "I was only trying to help. And you're not fat. You've gained a few pounds this summer. That's all. You'll lose them."

"Well, the articles are not helping. And I'm not a food addict. I just hate that I can't fit into my clothes."

"Why don't we go shopping before dinner? You could pick up a few things. I promise I won't say a word about dieting."

I know I need new clothes. I can't keep wearing the same pair of jeans and Dad's shirts. I should have gone shopping before school started. Mom suggested it a few times, but I kept saying no.

I used to love shopping before a new school year, but this year the thought makes me sick. I'm terrified of trying on clothes. What if I bump into someone from school while I'm standing beside a rack of giant-sized clothes? And how many sizes bigger am I anyway? One? Two? Three?

I wish someone could just whisk clothes over to me that make me look fabulous and skinny. I wish that I've only gone up one size. I wish I looked different. I can wish all I want, but I can't change anything right away. The seven-day diet will take time to work. In the meantime, I have to get new clothes. Not a lot. Just enough to keep me going till I lose weight.

"Okay," I agree.

Before I know it we're at Sanders department store. It's packed with kids and parents. I don't see anyone I know. We walk past the rack with small sizes. Zoe and Sarah could fit into these jeans, but not me. Not now.

We pass a rack with larger sizes. I look around. No one I know is here. I grab a few pairs of blue jeans in different sizes and zoom into a dressing room. Mom follows me and waits outside.

I lock the door. I stare at the jeans. Which one should I try on first?

I try on the largest pair. They're huge on me. Hooray! I'm not *that* big. Now for the real test. I grab the smallest pair. I slip one leg in and try to pull the jeans up. I wiggle and wiggle but they're stuck around my mid leg. I yank them off and slump down on the stool.

I stare at the jeans the next size up. "You'd better fit," I say. I slide one foot in, then the other. The jeans are halfway up and still moving. I yank them up higher. They're a little snug at the waist, but I can breathe. I can just manage to zip them up. I suck my gut in just a little and I can button them. I sit down. I don't think I'll split my pants but they're tight. I'd better not gain an ounce or they won't fit.

I pop out of the dressing room. "These work," I tell Mom. "Let's take two."

"You need shirts too. You can't keep borrowing Dad's."

We find two white shirts and one red shirt. They hang loose over my pants, but I know I'm not fooling anyone. Under these shirts, I'm still fat. I'm a blob, and everyone can see it.

"You look good in white and red," Mom says cheerfully.

"I look fat."

"You're not fat. You've gained some weight. It's no big deal. You'll lose the weight, although I'm not sure the fruit and veg diet is the best way to go."

"I'm trying this diet for now. Don't worry, I'll be fine. I won't faint or anything."

Mom says nothing. I know she thinks this diet is dumb.

At home, I hang up my new clothes. Then I eat a giant fruit salad. I used to love fruit, but now I'm beginning to hate it. And in two days I will only be able to eat bananas and milk. I'd rather have my teeth pulled.

That night I dream of roast chicken, grilled steak and stuffed turkey. I dream of hamburgers, pizza and mashed potatoes. Marshmallows dance through my dreams.

I swim in a tub of whipped cream. I dive into a hot fudge sundae. Jelly beans cascade down my face. They get tangled in my hair. Zoe tosses them at me. Jelly beans hit my nose and wake me up before my alarm blares. I pop my eyes open and shake the images of flying food out of my head. Then I remember breakfast.

Vegetables! How can I eat vegetables at 8:00 AM?

I slip into my new jeans and a white shirt and head downstairs. I open the fridge and stare at the vegetables filling the shelves and overflowing in all the bins. And then I see veggie juice! I can drink breakfast!

"I thought you might like that," Mom says, heading over to the coffeemaker.

"Yes! I love veggie juice. Thanks!"

I slurp down a glass. Then I cut up carrots and cucumbers. I pop them into a bag with baby tomatoes.

All the way to school, I think, One size down in a week. Two sizes down in two weeks. Soon you'll be back to your old weight. All you have to do is get through day two of the seven-day diet. It's one day at a time, and in the words of the diet— *you can do it*!

And I will!

"Never eat more than you can lift."

—Miss Piggy

chapter seven

I think of food in homeroom. I dream of food in English. I want food in history.

I even think about food during art, my favorite class. As I put the finishing touches on my ad for chocolate, Ms. Holmes tells us about our next project. She wants us to take an everyday object and give it a fresh visual twist.

I dab deep brown paint on my chocolate-bar picture and imagine a cookie tin as a jewelry box. I wonder what an empty bag of potato chips might look like as a puppet. I can almost see the mesh bag for oranges as a funky purse. Everything I think about is linked to food. Oh no! I am obsessed. I am a food addict!

Just stop thinking about food, I order myself. I need to choose something for my next project that has nothing to do with food. But all I can think about are things that relate to food—cans, bottles, baskets, cartons, crates.

At lunch, I sit with Denise and Carolyn. I eat my vegetables and try not to stare at Denise's tuna sandwich. I look away so I will not drool over Carolyn's strawberry yogurt. But when she pulls out her bag of chocolate-chip cookies, I eye it like I've never seen a cookie in my life. She offers me one, but I decline. I crunch down on a carrot. It tastes like wood.

Zoe saunters in with Sarah and Mia. I glance their way and catch Zoe pointing at me and laughing. Mia laughs, but Sarah doesn't. I can't imagine what Zoe is saying about me. But I know it's nasty.

I listen to Carolyn talk about her art project. She did an ad for hot dogs. Denise did one for gum.

"Gum is your favorite food?" I ask Denise. "Is gum a food?"

Denise laughs. "It was either gum or tuna. And I couldn't think of anything to make tuna visually exciting. Ms. Holmes wasn't crazy about my gum idea at first, but she finally said I could go ahead."

"So, what did you do?" I ask.

"I wrote *No time to exercise? Try gum. The tastiest way to exercise your mouth.*"

Carolyn and I howl. "That's great," I say.

"That's my kind of exercise," says Carolyn.

The bell rings. "Are you joining a club?" asks Carolyn as we head out of the lunchroom. "The deadline is Friday."

"I don't know," I say.

"We're thinking of becoming mentors," says Carolyn.

"What's that?" I ask.

"It's a new program called Girls Helping Girls. You meet with girls from middle school who have issues like family problems or body image because they're fat or...oops. Sorry," says Denise. "I wasn't thinking of you. Really. Anyway, you're not fat. You're just a little bigger than you were last year."

"It's okay. I know I'm fat, but I'm going to lose the weight. Why do you want to mentor?"

"It might be fun to help someone. I could tell the girl I mentor how I overcame hating my ugly nose."

"Your nose is not ugly," I say.

"Are you kidding?" says Denise. "Look at this hideous bump." Denise touches a tiny bump in the middle of her nose.

"It's hardly noticeable, and it's not hideous," I tell her.

"You're just saying that to be nice. I've wanted plastic surgery since I was five, but the doctor won't touch my nose till it's fully formed. He said I have to wait a few years. Meanwhile I'm stuck with it. So I've decided to ignore it, but you can't imagine how hard it is to live with a nose like mine. I see it every time I look in the mirror."

"Oh," I say. I really can't see the problem with Denise's nose.

The mentoring program sounds interesting. Only how can I help someone when I can't help myself? No matter how much I try to convince myself not to care about how fat I look or about Zoe's comments, I care.

And I hate dieting. I can't stand another vegetable. I'm seriously considering buying a chocolate bar after school. How can I be a mentor when I have no self-control?

Before I head home, I check out the bulletin board and scan the announcement about the mentoring program.

"Are you planning to help another fat girl?" someone says. It's Zoe.

I glare at her. She's standing with one hand on her hip and smirking at me. Her long hair is so straight, it looks ironed.

There's not an ounce of blobbiness about her. Even her arms are skinny.

"Why are you being so obnoxious?" I say.

"I'm not being obnoxious. I'm being helpful. I'm calling a spade a spade, or in your case a blob a blob. Get used to it. I'm not the only one in school who's noticed that you're obese."

Zoe turns around and prances off. She walks down the hall like a model on a runway.

I hurry toward home. Tears gush out of my eyes like I've sprung a leak.

When I get to the convenience store two blocks from my house, I wipe my eyes. Then I head inside and buy a chocolate bar.

For one block, I hold the chocolate bar in my hands. Then I stop and begin to unwrap it. But I don't eat it. I walk another half block and unwrap it some more. I still don't eat it. A few steps from home, I take a small bite. The chocolate tastes rich, dark, creamy. I'd forgotten how good chocolate tastes. I take another small bite. *Mmmm.* "I've missed you," I say out loud.

It takes all my willpower to stuff the rest of the chocolate bar into my backpack.

"The only way to lose weight is to check it as airline baggage."

—Peggy Ryan

chapter eight

There's a note on the kitchen table. *I'm out shopping for my book club meeting. It's at our house tonight. I thought I might bake cookies, but I won't if it bothers you. I'll get store-bought just in case. Love, Mom.*

I chug down a tall glass of veg juice and head to my room. No new articles about food addiction litter my bed. I sit down and pull the chocolate bar out of my backpack. I nibble a tiny bit. Then I stuff it into my desk drawer and start on my homework.

A half hour later, I hear the front door open. "I'm home!" Mom calls from the kitchen. "Would it bother you if I baked cookies?"

I head out of my room. "No. I'll even help."

"Are you sure?"

"Positive. I'll enjoy the smell of chocolate and get the buzz without the calories."

"Really?"

"Watch me."

Mom and I gather all the ingredients. We sift the flour, add salt and baking soda. We cream the sugar and butter and mix everything together. Then I drop chocolate chips into the soft dough and gently mix them in. When Mom isn't looking, I pop some chips into my mouth.

I watch the spoonfuls of warm batter spread into shapes in the oven. Oh no! They look like blobs. I snap the oven door shut.

Soon a sweet chocolaty smell fills the kitchen, and I pull the cookies out to cool.

"You're being very strong about this," says Mom.

"I'm determined to lose weight, and nothing will stop me. Not even chocolate-chip cookies."

"I'm sure one cookie won't spoil your diet," says Mom.

"Mom! Don't tempt me!" I say. "I have to be strict about this diet or it won't work."

"I'm sorry, Eve. I'm on your side. I shouldn't have suggested the cookie."

Why am I annoyed with my mother? She bought a whole fridge-full of fruit and vegetables to help me. She didn't force me to eat a quarter of a chocolate bar or the handful of chips. Maybe all the fruit and vegetables are making me insane! I need more protein, but I can't have that till day five of my diet.

After a supper of cooked carrots (no butter), steamed potatoes (no butter), spinach (no butter), lettuce and tomato salad (no dressing), I head to my room to work on my math homework. Ms. Murray is zipping through the material so quickly my head spins.

Soon I hear Mom's book-club friends come in. They comment on the delicious smell lingering through the house.

"It smells like chocolate perfume in here," says one of mom's friends.

Yes! Chocolate *is* the best perfume in the world. They should bottle it. Then I could just dab it on my skin and not eat it. But I'd miss eating it. It takes all my willpower not to charge into the kitchen and grab a cookie.

"Eve baked the cookies." I hear Mom tell her friends.

"What a lovely girl," says one of Mom's friends. "My Zoe never helps out. She does nothing at home but text message her friends."

Zoe's mother is in my mom's book club! I'm not stepping out of my room till they leave. I do not want to meet Zoe's mom. What would I say? Your daughter is obnoxious. She humiliates people. I hate her.

I start working on math. I can only figure out eight of the twelve questions. I stare at the four I can't figure out, but nothing comes to me. I pull out my chocolate bar. Maybe a little chocolate will help me think better. I take a bite, then another. I figure out one of the four questions. Maybe the chocolate is helping!

I eat some more. I've finished three quarters of the bar, but I'm still no further ahead with the other three math questions.

I stare at the questions for another twenty minutes and then give up. I'll ask the teacher tomorrow. I pull out the rest of the chocolate bar and eat the last few pieces as a reward for my efforts.

I enjoy every rich, melt-in-your-mouth bite, but when I finish I check the wrapper. I have just consumed three hundred and fifty calories. I can feel my gut getting blobbier by the minute.

"I keep trying to lose weight, but it keeps finding me."

—**Author Unknown**

chapter nine

I meet Carolyn on the way to school. Denise is sick with the flu. We talk about our art projects. Carolyn pulls out her ad for hot dogs to show me. It's great.

She has a man walking a dog down the street. A woman watches him while grilling sizzling hot dogs. The woman is grinning. The ad says:

Enjoy a hot dog today. One dog you don't have to walk.

"Ms. Holmes cracked up when she saw it," she says.

I tell Carolyn the slogan for my chocolate-bar ad.

"Fabulous," she says. "How's your diet going?"

"Not so fabulous. I got through day one, which was all fruit, and day two, which was all vegetables. Today I can eat a mix of fruit and vegetables, and I'll be fine. But tomorrow will be hell. Tomorrow I can only eat bananas and drink milk."

"That's disgusting." Carolyn wrinkles her nose. "How will you stand it?"

"I don't know if I can."

"Try another diet. There are thousands out there," she says. "My mother tries a new one every month."

I nod. "I might have to. This one is killing me."

Carolyn pats me on the back. "I could never stick to your diet for even one day unless I was forced to at gunpoint. You have amazing self-control."

I laugh. If Carolyn knew that I ate an entire chocolate bar and a bunch of chocolate chips, she might not be amazed at my willpower. But then again, I did stick to about 95 percent of the diet. "Are you still thinking of being a mentor?" I ask her.

"I'm going to the meeting tomorrow after school. They'll tell us more about the program and pair us with the girl we're mentoring. I hope her problem isn't anything too weird, like having eleven toes. Why don't you come to the meeting too?"

"I don't know. I've never done anything like this before. I don't know how to help someone with something I've never had."

"Like eleven toes?" says Carolyn.

"Yes, I can't imagine what that would be like."

"Well, they'll probably give us suggestions on how to deal with the girl we're mentoring. It should be fine."

As we trek up the stairs into school, Carolyn groans, "I have to run. I need help from Ms. Murray with math."

"Did you have trouble with questions nine to twelve?" I ask as she turns down the hall.

"I had trouble with questions one to twelve. I'm hopeless in math. But luckily I'm a whiz at hot dogs!"

We wave and I hurry to homeroom. I slide into my seat beside Sarah. She doesn't lift her head from her book.

"What are you reading?" I ask.

Sarah raises her eyes. "*Vampire Dreams*."

"Is it good?"

Sarah nods, and a less-than-quarter smile crosses her face. Her smiles have shrunk to almost nothing now. Her eyes shoot back to her book.

"What's going on, Sarah?" I blurt out.

Sarah looks up. "Nothing," she says. Her eyes are cold and distant.

"It's not nothing. I thought we were friends. Are you angry at me? Did I say something?"

Sarah rolls her eyes. "Don't be so sensitive, Eve. Things change. We're in high school. We're all meeting new people."

Her eyes return to her book. I feel like she's slammed a door in my face.

I know she's dropped me. But why? Is it because I'm fat? Is it because Zoe is skinny and perfect? Is it because Zoe is friends with Mia—who knows everybody at school?

I feel a lump in my throat. I try to swallow it before it turns into tears. I can't let Sarah see how much this hurts.

I'm sorry I said anything to her. I wish I could grab my words back, but they're gone. And so is our friendship.

I pass the bulletin board on the way to my next class. I read the information on the mentoring program again.

GIRLS HELPING GIRLS
Help girls struggling with difficult times. Discover how helping others become stronger and more confident will make you stronger and more confident too.

Trained counselors will guide and assist you with any issues you may encounter.

Why not? I think. Maybe I'll be teamed up with another fat girl and together we can get skinny. Maybe helping someone else with their problems will make me feel better.

I can't stand the way I feel now. At least Carolyn and Denise are around. And they'll be in the mentoring program. As long as Zoe and Sarah don't show up, it might be fun.

And if I don't like it, I'll leave.

"The leading cause of death among fashion models is falling through street grates."

—Dave Barry

chapter ten

As soon as the last bell rings, I head for room twelve, where the mentoring program is being held. I look for Carolyn, but I don't see her. I haven't seen her since lunch. She said she was feeling hot and dizzy. I wonder if she caught Denise's flu.

There are ten girls and two women in the room. I don't know anyone, although two of the girls look familiar. I've probably seen them in the hall. Most look like they're in grade eleven or twelve. There's no sign of Zoe or Sarah. Today is the tryout for cheerleaders, so they're probably there.

One of the women walks to the center of the room. She's short with straight brown hair, red glasses and large green eyes.

When we're all seated, she begins. "My name is Joan Hawkins and I'm delighted to see you all. Let me tell you about our program. We team girls in high school up with girls in middle school who are having a tough time. It helps the middle school girls to know that there's someone they can talk to and feel comfortable with no matter what they're going through. And I know that by supporting someone else, each of you will feel good too."

Joan smiles. Then she continues. "When I was in middle school, my parents split up. My mom, my brother and I moved six times. It was difficult starting a new school and trying to make new friends. I threw up every morning before I went to school. But I was lucky. When I felt low, I talked to my cousin Mary, who was in high school.

Mary's understanding and support made all the difference. Not everyone has a Mary in her life. But each of you can be like my cousin and make a difference for the girl you mentor."

I glance around the room. Many of the girls are nodding. Some are smiling.

The other woman walks to the front of the room. She has long gray hair tied back in a ponytail. She's wearing dangling earrings and an armful of silver bracelets. "I'm Linda Day," she says. "Joan and I will be here to support you whenever you need us. If you run into a tricky situation, you can always speak to us. You're not alone either."

Linda looks around the room and smiles. "The mentoring program was started a few years ago, and we've already had great success. Tonight Joan and I will chat with each of you individually to see how we can best match you with a middle-school girl. Next week we'll team you up with the girls you'll be mentoring. I'll start with the front row and Joan will start at the back.

Please feel free to have drinks and cookies while you wait. I baked the cinnamon cookies myself."

As Joan and Linda begin to speak to the girls in the room, other girls rush to the front to grab drinks and cookies.

I eye the two plates piled high with cookies. I love homemade cinnamon cookies. After nothing but vegetables and fruit all day, I'm starving. Those cookies look delicious. But I'm the second girl waiting in the back row, so Joan will be speaking to me soon. I'd better not get up.

I pull out my history textbook and try to read ahead, but my eyes boomerang back to the plate of cookies.

One cookie won't make me fat. I stand up to get one. Then I quickly sit down. What am I thinking? That's how it starts— one cookie, then another. Pretty soon I'll eat ten. Forget about the cookies, I tell myself. Read your history book.

Joan and the girl beside me talk on and on. I read a paragraph, but my eyes are drawn back to the cookies. I need a cookie. I need to eat something.

I stand up again. But before I can leave the back row, it's my turn to speak to Joan. Saved by the mentoring program already!

"So tell me a little about why you want to mentor a middle-school girl," Joan asks me.

"I hope that by helping someone else I can deal with my own problems better," I tell her.

"Good. You just have to be careful to focus on the middle-school girl and her problems, not on your own. But people who help others often help themselves."

"Will the girl have a problem like mine? You know, a weight issue."

"We try to match girls we feel can help each other," Joan explains. "The particular issue isn't what's important. Sometimes it's better to mentor someone who has a totally different problem than yours. So what do you think? Do you want to mentor, Eve?"

"Yes. I'd like to try."

Joan nods and I sign her list. She hands me a brochure. I need to get permission from my parents, but that won't be a problem. They'll like the idea that I'm helping someone.

I walk out of the meeting glad that I signed up for the program.

And even more glad that I didn't eat a cookie.

"The first thing you lose in a diet is your sense of humor."

—**Author Unknown**

chapter eleven

Mom and Dad love the mentoring idea. They sign the permission papers over their supper of roast chicken, corn on the cob, mashed potatoes and salad.

I watch them sign it over my supper of boiled potatoes, corn (no butter), salad (no dressing) and melon. Tonight's supper isn't bad. Tomorrow will be terrible. Bananas and milk. I groan at the thought. Mom asks what's wrong. "Nothing," I say. I don't want them to know how much I hate my diet.

I feel like I've been dieting for months, not just three days. I think about food all the time. I never used to think about food. I just ate it.

The next morning I create a banana and milk smoothie for breakfast. It's not great but it's drinkable.

"Are you sure you want to continue with this diet?" Mom asks as I grab two bananas for lunch.

"I have to," I tell Mom. "I need to get back to my old weight."

"But fad diets don't work, and they're unhealthy."

"This isn't really a fad diet. Fad diets make you eat only one food or really weird food like cabbage or blueberries all day. This one doesn't. Well, except for today. Today is weird. But the weekend will be normal. I can eat beef, chicken or fish with vegetables. And I'm pretty sure the diet is working already. My pants feel looser."

"Where did you find this diet?"

"I saw it on the Internet. Gotta go."

Before Mom can give me more reasons my diet is stupid, I'm out the door.

As I hurry down the street, I check my pants. They're not really looser, but I had to say something to get Mom off my case.

In homeroom Sarah talks to me for a few minutes, but it's like she's talking to someone she's met on a bus for the first time.

In art, I hear that Carolyn and Denise are both sick with the flu. I'm on my own at lunch.

As soon as I walk into the lunchroom, I see Sarah with Zoe. I hurry toward a bench at the other end of the lunchroom. I slip in beside a bunch of grade-eleven girls.

I eat my two bananas quickly. I consider buying milk, but the thought of drinking plain milk makes me ill. Maybe day four of this diet is to test your willpower. If you can survive a day of bananas and milk, you can survive anything.

What now? I can't just sit here. I have to go somewhere till my next class. But where?

Not the bathroom. There are too many gross possibilities there. How about the library? It smells better than the bathroom, and I can read till the bell rings. I dump my banana peels in the garbage and head for the library.

I find a quiet corner and grab a mystery from a rack. For fifteen minutes I forget about food, Zoe or Sarah.

I try listening to every word the teachers say in my next two classes, but all I can think about is how hungry I am. By the end of the day, I know I can't stand another bite of a banana or a sip of white milk.

On the way home from my school, I buy chocolate milk. I know I'm cheating, but chocolate milk *is* milk. It just has a little sugar, and it won't make me barf.

But what about supper? I cannot eat another banana. I decide to skip the rest of day four on the diet and zip to day five. I have no choice. I need real food. When I tell Mom, she doesn't make a crack about crazy fad diets. She just says, "Dinner will be ready at seven."

For dinner I feast on leftover roast chicken and vegetables. I never realized before how delicious leftover chicken could taste. When I finish my chicken and vegetables, I reach for a chocolate-chip cookie, but at the last minute I resist. I decide to save my calories for tomorrow. It's my grandmother's birthday and there will be cake. Grandma would be insulted if I didn't eat a piece of her birthday cake. It will be double-fudge chocolate—Grandma's favorite and mine.

Grandma's party is at our house. Mom and I spend the morning making little sandwiches and dicing fruit for salad.

When Mom pulls the cake out of the oven, the kitchen smells wonderful. I can't wait to taste the cake.

By the time I have to set the table, the double-fudge cake is iced and waiting on the counter. It is impossible for me to ignore. I want to plunge my finger into the center of it and lick the rich icing off my fingers like I did when I was a kid. I've never wanted a piece of cake so much in my life.

At noon Grandma and Aunt Betty arrive at our house.

As we nibble on the sandwiches, I stare at the cake. It looks luscious. I want it now! We eat the little sandwiches, and Grandma opens her presents. All I can think about the whole time is eating the double-fudge cake.

Finally Grandma opens her presents and says, "Let's have cake!" She blows out the seven candles—one for each decade of her life. Then she cuts a slice for Mom, Dad and Aunt Betty.

She's about to cut one for me. It's going to be a huge piece. Grandma always gives me a huge helping of our favorite cake. I have to stop her. If a giant slab of cake lands on my plate, I'll eat it all—every scrumptious crumb and gooey bite.

"Wait, Grandma!" I say. "I can only have a small piece. I'm on a diet."

"Diet! You? Nonsense," says Grandma. She puts her arm around my shoulder.

"You don't need to diet, Eve." Grandma pulls me over to the front hall. "Look in the mirror, Eve. You are gorgeous just the way you are. A few extra pounds actually suit you. You have a wonderful smile and lovely eyes."

Mom walks over. "Grandma's right. You are beautiful just the way you are. If you want to lose a few pounds, go ahead, but one piece of cake won't make a difference. You've been good all week."

"And dieting is torture," says Grandma. "You don't have to eat like crazy, but you don't have to torture yourself either. You only live once. You might as well enjoy every minute."

Grandma is right. Dieting is torture.

Mom is wrong. I haven't been good about my diet all week. I've cheated.

But I'm not any fatter. My new clothes fit. I glance in the hall mirror again. I don't look bad in my new jeans and red shirt. A little rounder in the middle, but I am not a blob.

I am going to eat some cake.

"If you don't run your life, someone else will."

—John Atkinson

chapter twelve

On Sunday night I decide to abandon the You Can Do It in Seven Days diet. I can't live through another week of being snubbed by Sarah, sneered at by Zoe, learning impossible math, meeting the girl I'll mentor and dealing with this diet too. Instead I'll just eat less. I almost survived a whole day of bananas and milk, so eating less will be a piece of cake.

Carolyn and Denise are back at school on Monday. All through lunch we talk about teachers, homework and art. Even though they're best friends, they include me. It's great not having to hide in the bathroom.

After our last class, the three of us meet in front of the mentoring room. Inside, a bunch of middle-school girls are standing near the refreshments, drinking juice and eating cookies. They stare at us when we come in. One girl is hugely overweight. I wonder if that will be the girl I'll mentor.

Another girl has a strange red scar on her face. I've never seen anyone with a scar like that. I try not to stare at her. Beside her is a girl with a big nose. Denise's nose is a polka dot compared to this girl's nose. Another girl is in a wheelchair. The rest of the girls have nothing obviously different about them, although one girl is biting her nails so hard I think she's going to chew them right off.

The meeting is called to order after a short introduction. Joan and Linda announce the partners. Carolyn gets Helene, the girl with the big nose. Denise gets Nicole, the overweight girl, and I get the girl with the red scar. Her name is Stephanie.

I walk over to her. "Hi. I'm Eve."

She folds her hands across her chest and scowls. "I didn't want to come here but my mom made me," she blurts out. She glares at me as if she's challenging me to take her on.

Now what? How do I get her to talk? How do I get her to want to be here? How do I mentor her? Her problem is probably her scar, but how do I bring that up? The material Joan and Linda gave us said not to avoid the issues but to take our cue from the girl we're mentoring. Well, Stephanie's cue is "lay off me and don't ask me anything."

"So how do you like school?" I ask.

"I hate it and it hates me," she barks.

Now what?

"It's hard to start a new year. This is my first year in high school and I'm finding it difficult to get used to," I say.

"Is that 'cause you're fat?"

My mouth hangs open. I can't believe Stephanie just called me fat. Neither can Joan, who's standing nearby.

I'm so stunned I can't speak. I want to run out of the room. Why did I say yes to mentoring? How can I help someone who's so mean and angry?

But I don't run. "I'm not fat," I say. "I gained some weight over the summer, and I'm not happy about that. It makes me uncomfortable, especially when people say rotten things to me. Like you just did."

I can see Joan from the corner of my eye. She is grinning. I'm glad I spoke up. I'm glad I called a spade a spade—or, as Zoe would say, a blob a blob.

Stephanie is silent for a minute. Then she mutters, "Sorry."

"Let's start again," I say.

Stephanie shrugs, but the look on her face softens. "I'm such a loser," she mumbles.

"You're not a loser, and I'm not a loser either. How did you get the scar?"

I regret my words immediately. Stephanie hasn't volunteered anything and here I'm asking her about her scar.

Stephanie looks startled by my question.

"It's not a scar. It's a birthmark. It's called a port-wine stain and I hate it."

"It's not...," I begin. Then I stop. I'm about to say it's not the worst thing in the world. I'm about to tell her that it would be worse if she was missing a leg or had cancer. It's true, those things are worse than being overweight or having a scar. But I just can't say it. I'd sound like I'm lecturing.

"It stinks feeling different," I say.

Joan is beaming at me. I know I'm saying the right things.

"You're not kidding it stinks," Stephanie suddenly yells. Her face hardens. "Being fat is nothing compared to my life. Everyone hates me. Even my dad. No one knows how I feel. No one."

Then Stephanie runs out of the room.

"Laughter is the shortest distance between two people."

—Victor Borge

chapter thirteen

I feel like someone has socked me in the stomach. Everyone heard Stephanie scream. Everyone saw her charge out of the room. I don't know where to go or what to do.

Joan hurries over to me. "I'm a failure at mentoring," I groan.

"You said all the right things," says Joan. "Stephanie is angry, but not at you. Anything could have set her off."

"She'll never come back now," I say.

"You never know." Joan pats me on the shoulder. "I'll be right back, and we'll talk more."

By now everyone has turned back to their partners. They're talking and laughing like nothing weird just happened. All the other high-school girls are having nice friendly chats with the middle graders they're mentoring. I'm the only one who made my student so angry she flew out the door. I flop down on a chair near the refreshments. I stare at the cookies. I'm desperate for a cookie. Just one wouldn't hurt. I stretch my hand out toward the plate.

"Don't eat it," someone barks at me. I spin around. It's Stephanie. "You don't want to get any fatter."

"You came back!" I say.

"I had to come back. I left my bag on the chair."

"I'm sorry if I said the wrong thing. And you're right. I'm not going to eat that cookie, even though I really, really, really want to."

Stephanie looks at me. Then she begins to laugh. She laughs so hard she shakes.

"What's so funny?" I ask her.

"You're mentoring me and you need mentoring yourself. You should have seen the way you looked at the cookies. You were like a wolf eyeing a pig."

"A wolf eyeing a pig!" I repeat. "That's so..." I start to laugh. I don't know why it strikes me funny to be compared to a wolf. Maybe it's better than being compared to a pig. I just know that I can't stop laughing.

Denise and Nicole stare at us. Carolyn and Helene stare at us. Everyone stares at us, but we can't stop laughing.

Joan walks to the front of the room. "I'm glad to see that everyone is getting along so well," she says. Then she turns to us. "Some of you seem to be getting along especially well. Care to share the joke, girls?" Joan grins at us.

"I'd share it," I say. "If I knew what it was."

"Yeah," says Stephanie. "I don't know why we're laughing."

"Well, whatever the reason, laughing is a good thing," says Joan. "Let's all meet back here on Wednesday for more laughs, talk and refreshments."

"But no more cookies for you," says Stephanie, wagging her finger in my face.

I make a fake annoyed face at her. I feel better than I have in days. I don't even want the cookie.

We walk out together and promise to meet back on Wednesday. We exchange phone numbers.

I feel amazing all the way home. I can't wait for Wednesday.

After supper I google *port-wine stain*. The first site I check out explains that it's a birthmark caused by swollen blood vessels. About three in a thousand people have one. If it's that common, how come Stephanie's the first person I've ever met who has one? Maybe if I'd seen more port-wine stains, I wouldn't have been so startled when I first saw hers.

The site also says that most of the time port-wine stains appear on people's faces. It mentions that some people have emotional problems because of the stigma attached to looking different. Who could blame them? The stain is right there where you can't miss it. Like my round stomach.

Some of the treatments for port-wine stains are freezing, surgery, radiation, laser treatment and tattooing. Tattooing?

I wonder how they do that. Tattoos are actually like a stain but in a shape you choose. Tattooing is cool these days, so why isn't a port-wine stain cool? Wouldn't it be amazing if it became cool? Wouldn't it be something if those of us who don't have a stain became the weird people?

I wonder if I should tell Stephanie what I'm thinking.

Probably not.

On Tuesday I eat cereal for breakfast, and it's wonderful not to eat bananas or drink vegetable juice. Sarah talks to me a little in homeroom, and I hardly care if she's not my friend anymore. At lunch Zoe isn't around and I'm relieved.

I hang out with Carolyn and Denise, and they tease me about how Stephanie and I stopped the mentoring meeting with our hysterical laughter.

On Tuesday night, I eat a small bowl of Mom's spaghetti with a large bowl of salad. I savor each spaghetti strand. I love the flavor of the Parmesan on top. I only have one cookie for dessert. It's a large cookie, but it's only one. Mom compliments me on my "intelligent" diet.

"I'm not on a diet," I tell her. "I'm just trying not to eat too much."

"Well, I'm proud of you. Diet or no diet. You're on your way."

All through classes on Wednesday, I don't think about food. I think about my latest art project and seeing Stephanie again.

I hurry to the mentoring meeting right after class. All the girls are there. Everyone is talking and nibbling on refreshments. There's a friendly buzz in the room.

I look around for Stephanie, but I don't see her.

"Where's Stephanie?" I ask Joan.

Joan winces. "Her mom called and said Stephanie wasn't coming back."

"What? Never?"

Joan shakes her head. She doesn't say the word *never* but I know that's what she is thinking.

> "Someone's opinion of you doesn't have to become your reality."
>
> **—Les Brown**

chapter fourteen

"I don't get it."

"Neither do I. You two seemed to be hitting it off so well," said Joan.

"Did her mom say why she isn't coming back?"

"No. She just said Stephanie didn't want to come anymore."

"I thought we were becoming friends. I thought we were able to talk. I thought..."

A donut-sized lump forms in my throat. I try to swallow it, but it's stuck there like a sticky piece of dough.

Joan gives me a hug. "You were wonderful. It's not your fault. You can't win everyone. Sometimes people's sadness goes too deep."

I remember Stephanie's comment about her dad hating her. "You're probably right," I say, "but I still wish I could have helped her. I might as well go home."

"Don't go. We'll figure something out. Maybe we can pair you up with someone else."

"No, thanks. I've had enough."

I hurry toward the outside door. I don't understand it. Stephanie was beginning to feel comfortable with me. She gave me her phone number. I know she wanted us to meet again. So what happened between Monday and tonight? It was only two days. She has to be upset about something. Maybe something happened at school.

I open the front door and walk down the first step and then I stop. I can't let Stephanie quit. I can't let me quit.

I turn around and run back inside. I race down the hall and into the meeting room. I'm out of breath when I approach Joan.

"Can I borrow your cell phone?" I ask her.

"Sure."

I fish Stephanie's phone number out of my wallet and tap in her number.

The phone rings five times. Then someone answers. I know it's Stephanie immediately.

"Hi, Stephanie." I speak quickly so she won't hang up. "It's Eve."

"I don't want to talk to you."

"Then just listen. Please come back to the meeting. Without you, I'll eat every cookie in the room. I need your help. Desperately."

I can hear Stephanie breathing, so I know she's still there.

"Eating cookies when you're fat is stupid," she finally says.

"I know. I know. I have no willpower. I'm total mush when it comes to food, especially cookies, ice cream and chocolate."

"I don't like cookies that much, but I feel that way about potato chips."

"I like potato chips but I don't love them. Not passionately. Not the way I feel about chocolate. So will you come? Don't make me beg."

Silence. Then finally, "Okay. I guess I can come. I had a bad day on Tuesday. I didn't go to school today."

"Are you going to school tomorrow?"

"I don't know."

"But you'll come to the meeting at the high school on Friday, right?"

"Okay," she says.

"Promise?"

"I promise if you promise not to eat any cookies today."

"I promise."

"I'll ask Joan and Linda and all your friends if you kept your word, you know."

"I'll keep my word. See ya."

"See ya."

I hand Joan back her phone.

"I'm impressed," she says.

"Me too," says Linda.

"I'll be more impressed if she shows up on Friday," I tell them.

The mentoring meeting is over five minutes later. All the way home I wonder if Stephanie will come on Friday. I'm sure now that something awful happened to her at school. The next two days are busy with homework. I don't think about diets or food. I'm not eating too much or too little. I'm just eating the way I used to—before this summer. Something must be working because I've lost a pound. Okay, a pound isn't much. I have a lot more to go, but it's better than gaining a pound.

I'm having lunch on Friday with Denise and Carolyn when Zoe, Sarah and Mia sit at a nearby table. I hear Zoe say, "She's not just a blob, she's a total suck-up. My mother thinks she's *wonderful*. It's disgusting."

Sarah looks stiff and uncomfortable. Mia says nothing. But they both listen to Zoe go on about me.

"What's Zoe ranting about? Since when did you suck up to her mother?" asks Carolyn.

I shrug. "I've never met her mother. She's in my mom's book club, but I've never even talked to her. I don't know what Zoe is talking about. She keeps insulting me, and I have no idea why."

"Zoe and her mom don't get along. They scream at each other a lot," says Denise.

"But what does that have to do with me?" I say. And then I remember how Zoe's mom complimented me at the book club meeting. What if Zoe hates me because her mom compares us? But even if it's true, what can I do about it?

After class, I hurry to my locker to put my books away. As I near it, I see something stuck to the front of my locker. I gasp. It's a picture of a fat lady from a circus. Beside it there's a small mirror taped to my locker door. There's a note under the picture. It says: *Does she look familiar? Look in the mirror. She's YOU!*

There's no signature, but I know who wrote it.

I rip the picture off my locker. I tear it into tiny pieces and dump it into the garbage.

I hear giggling from behind the lockers down the hall. I lift the mirror carefully off my locker and turn in the direction of the giggles.

"Thanks for the mirror. I needed one!" I say.

The giggles stop.

I walk down the hall to the mentoring meeting and open the door.

"No one can make you feel inferior without your permission."

—Eleanor Roosevelt

chapter fifteen

Stephanie is talking to Joan. I rush over.

"Great to see you," I say.

"So, did you eat any cookies on Wednesday?" she asks.

"Ask Joan. Ask Linda. Ask Denise, Helene, Carolyn or Nicole. Ask anyone and they'll tell you I didn't. Not a single cookie, and I even lost a pound."

"A pound isn't a whole lot. Two pounds would be better."

"Boy, you sure can crush a girl's ego," I tell her. "I bet I'll lose another pound soon. Maybe tonight."

We both laugh.

We banter like that for a while.

I wish I knew how to bring up what kept Stephanie out of school. I want to ask her if she went to school today, but I don't. She doesn't volunteer anything.

Joan calls the meeting to order and suggests that everyone plan to do something together outside of the meeting. "You could go bowling, take a walk or see a movie."

Stephanie mentions a new film about a teen who turns into a witch and develops secret powers she has to hide from her family. We decide to go on Sunday for a matinee.

As we leave the meeting, we agree to confirm our plans on the phone tomorrow morning.

"I'm really glad you came today," I tell her.

"And I'm really glad you didn't eat any cookies."

"I didn't even want one. It's amazing. See how much your nagging helped me?"

"Yeah, right," says Stephanie, grinning. For the first time I notice that she has dimples.

Early Saturday morning the phone rings. I answer before Mom. There's a woman's voice at the other end of the phone.

"I'm Mary McCall," she says. "Stephanie's mom."

"Is Stephanie okay?" I ask.

"She's fine. Well, not completely fine, but she's not sick. She doesn't know I'm calling you."

My heart starts to pound. Have I said something to upset Stephanie? Is she going to back out of going to the movie?

"Stephanie's been crying for two days. Something happened at school, and for some reason she's convinced now that her dad and I split up because of her. It's only been a month since her father moved out. Of course, Stephanie has nothing to do with it. I was glad she went to the meeting with you, but now she's refusing to get out of bed."

"Oh." I don't know what to say.

"She likes you, Eve."

Mrs. McCall is asking me for help. How can I help her? I don't know what to say to Stephanie.

"Can I talk to Stephanie?" I ask.

"Why don't you call her in an hour? She's still asleep. She hardly slept last night."

"Okay. I'll call."

"I really appreciate what a friend you've become to Stephanie. She used to have a lot of friends, but since she started middle school it's been tough."

Mrs. McCall hangs up. I sit cross-legged on my bed and try to think of something to say to Stephanie. I reread the mentoring notes three times. Anything I think of sounds like I'm preaching. Saying everything will be fine isn't enough.

She must feel incredibly sad that her parents are splitting up. Feeling she's responsible is terrible. Being a few pounds overweight is nothing compared to that. But what can I do to make things easier for Stephanie? Are any words enough?

I check the clock. I have to call her in a few minutes, and my mind is a blank.

I dial her number. The phone rings and rings. Finally Mrs. McCall answers. "I'll get Stephanie for you," she says. Then she whispers, "Good luck and thanks."

My hands are shaking as I wait for Stephanie to come to the phone. I don't want to let her mom down.

"Hi, Eve," says Stephanie. She sounds distant and hesitant. Not unfriendly, just far away.

"I wanted to set up the time we'll meet for the movie. Do you want me to pick you up at your house so we can go together?"

"I...I...don't know if I can go," she stammers.

"Please go," I say. "It's been a crazy week at school. This movie will cheer me up." I'm almost begging.

"Well...okay...but I'd rather my mom drove me," she says.

"Great. Witches with magic powers always cheer me up. They make me wish I had magic powers."

"What kind of magic powers would you want?" she asks.

"The power to turn nasty people into toads or ants or cockroaches. I'd love to do that to Zoe."

"Who's Zoe?" Stephanie asks.

"A girl who left a picture of a fat lady at the circus on my locker on Friday," I said. "There was a horrible note too, about how fat I am."

"What did you do?"

"I ripped the note up and kept the mirror. I knew she was hiding behind the lockers so she could see my reaction. I thanked her for her mirror."

"You're kidding. That's awesome."

"It felt good. I can't always think of the right thing to say, but I did then. See you at one forty-five. I'll buy the tickets early so we can go in as soon as you get there. It's my treat."

"Thanks."

"I'm glad we're going together. I can't wait to see how that witch uses her powers!"

"Feeling good is better than
a hot-fudge sundae."

—Eve Richards

chapter sixteen

I arrive at the movie theater at 1:15 PM.
There's already a line. I see some kids from
my school and some middle-school kids. I bet
some of them are from Stephanie's school.
I hope there are no kids who've been
tormenting her here. I hope going to the
movies is not going to be a disaster.

I wave to one of the girls from my
art class as she hurries into the theater.
I buy our tickets and wait for Stephanie.

She's not there at 1:45. She's not there at 1:50. Then 1:55 passes, and still there's no Stephanie. I'm starting to think she's not coming. I wonder if she panicked about going out at the last minute. And then a car drives up. Stephanie jumps out.

"I'll pick you up after the movie," says her mom before she drives away.

Stephanie and I dash into the packed theater. We sit in the second row from the back.

Stephanie sinks into her seat.

"I guess there's no time for popcorn," I whisper as the theater darkens.

"Do you know how many calories there are in a bag of movie popcorn?" she says.

"You sound like my mother. I wasn't going to have any popcorn. I wanted to know if you wanted some."

"Nah. I always get those little kernels stuck between my teeth. Then I spend the rest of the movie trying to get them out with my tongue."

"Me too, or I get bits stuck in my throat and I feel like I'm going to gag. I keep clearing my throat and guzzling down water."

We stop talking when the movie starts.

It's a silly movie, but it's fun. I love how Ellie, the girl who's a witch, uses her powers to get revenge on Cleo, the popular girl at school who belittles her. Cleo has a perfect body, a perky nose, long straight blond hair and blue eyes. Ellie gives Cleo a humpback.

When Cleo complains, Ellie says, "If you wear the right outfit, it won't show much."

That cracks Stephanie up. She laughs so hard that she holds her stomach. I'm laughing too, and before we know it, the movie is over.

"That was so good," says Stephanie as the lights go back on.

We walk out of the theater talking about the movie. As we reach the outside door, someone taps me on the shoulder. I turn. It's Zoe. Mia and Sarah are with her.

"Hi, Eve," says Zoe. "It's too bad you can't find anyone your own age to go to the movies with."

I glance at Sarah. She cringes but says nothing.

"Stephanie meet Zoe. Zoe is the girl I told you about. Zoe likes to leave nasty notes for people on their lockers."

Zoe looks like I've smacked her in the face but she recovers quickly.

"You think you're so smart, Eve? But you're not. My mom said you baked the cookies for her book club. You probably made them so you could stuff your face with them. No wonder you have a weight issue."

"It's true. I make amazing cookies. You should try some. Chocolate cookies make people smile. You could use a smile," I say.

I see Sarah stifling a laugh. "Did you like the movie?" Sarah asks me.

"Yes. Some of the characters reminded me of people I know. Cleo reminded me a little of you, Zoe."

Zoe glares at me.

"I have to go, Eve," says Stephanie. "My mom's waiting."

"I'll come with you. See you, Sarah. See you, Zoe and Mia."

"See you," says Sarah, and for the first time since school began Sarah gives me a real smile. It's almost a "Let's be friends again" smile. I smile back, but I don't know if I can ever be friends with her again.

Stephanie and I look for her mom's car in the parking lot.

"Do you want to come over to my house for supper?" Stephanie asks as her mom drives up.

"Sure."

"Great," says Stephanie. "I haven't had a friend over since...my dad left."

"I'm sorry to hear about your dad," I say.

"It's okay. I still see him. He called last night, and he's taking me out for supper next weekend."

"That's terrific," I say. "By the way, I'm glad we went to the movies."

"Me too. And I really think you've lost weight, Eve. You don't need to lose all that much anyway. But I bet you've lost more than two pounds."

I laugh. "Maybe I have—but even if I haven't, I feel good and that's better than losing weight. It's even better than eating a hot-fudge sundae. And take it from me, that's saying a lot."

Frieda Wishinsky takes her inspiration for *Blob* from the summer she worked as a counselor. She worked with some tough teens and cheered herself up by visiting the local Dairy Queen—often. Frieda is the award-winning author of over forty books for young people, including *Queen of the Toilet Bowl* in the Orca Currents series. Frieda lives in Toronto, Ontario.

orca *currents*

The following is an excerpt from
another exciting Orca Currents novel,
Struck by Deb Loughead.

Struck
Deb Loughead

978-1-55469-211-8 $9.95 pb
978-1-55469-212-5 $16.95 lib

Claire's life is in need of a major overhaul. She's failing math, her depressed mother won't get off the couch and the boy of her dreams is dating her nemesis Lucy. Just as Claire is wishing her life were better, lightning strikes. Soon her life changes, and Claire has everything she thought she ever wanted. It doesn't take long before Claire starts to worry that the cost of good fortune may be too high.

chapter one

It was one of those days when you don't even want to step outside—a bleak and windy Sunday in November. And of course my mom asked me to run to the store. She was craving clam chowder. *Clam chowder*, of all the stupid things! The New England kind. Not the Manhattan kind. And she wanted it, like, right away.

"There's some money in my purse, Claire. It's in the hallway on the table."

She wasn't even looking at me. She was flopped on the sofa with the clicker in her hand, flipping through the channels.

"Why can't *you* go, Mom? I'm kinda busy right now." *Why don't you get out of the house yourself for a change? You're getting so fat and lazy!* That's what I really wanted to snap back at her. But I didn't want to hurt her feelings. They'd been hurt enough lately.

"My arthritis is acting up again," she said. "My feet are killing me." This was her usual excuse. She used to cope with it and just carry on with her day—before Dad left, that is. Ever since then, she'd been housebound. And at fifteen, I didn't want a stay-at-home mom anymore. She needed to get out and get on with her life. But Dad packed her zest for life into his suitcase and took it with him. I didn't miss him at all, but she sure did.

Besides, I had better things to do that day than running errands for my mom. I had a math test to study for, and I needed to pull up my lousy marks. I also wanted to memorize a dramatic monologue for an audition at school. Oh, and there was daydreaming about Eric. That was always a priority. He was stuck in my head like a burr on your sleeve. There was nothing I could do to shake him off.

The only problem was, I didn't stand a chance. Eric was going out with my number one rival, Lucy. She was one of the most popular girls at school—one of those girls that you never feel cool enough to be friends with. Lucy wins at everything by hardly even trying, and she is always surrounded by a flock of friends. I'd secretly wished she would be my friend. But Lucy and I had never been close the way my best friend Seema and I were. Lucy and I talked sometimes, during drama and English class, and said "hi" in the halls, but that was about it.

Sometimes I had fantasies about putting that girl out of *my* misery. But that's all they ever were—crazy, twisted fantasies. Like, what if she walked a little too close to the edge of the stage one day and "accidentally" fell off and broke her ankle? I'd have to take over her role in a play—and I would totally rock the part. I wished I could control my vivid imagination, but it just wasn't happening.

I left for the store just as the first fat raindrops started to pelt my head. A mushy mixture of rain and snow, they felt like icy needles on my scalp. I hurried along the sidewalk, thinking about my mom the entire time. I thought about the way she didn't care about herself and about her lack of interest in *anything* these days. She'd turned into a boring lump. I would never let my life turn out like hers. I would never be like her.

Dad had ditched us a few months earlier because of what he called a "midlife crisis." Mom seemed to be curling into herself like a snail into its shell. She hardly ever showered, she hardly ever moved. I didn't miss Dad's lousy moods or his hair-trigger temper. Or the way he used to grab Mom by the arm and squeeze until he left a bruise. I sure couldn't figure out why she missed it.

Her face was always a blank mask, her eyes dull and staring. She was always sighing. Oh, and asking me to run to the store to pick up random stuff that she had a craving for. Sometimes it was weird, like a jar of pickled herring, or a box of instant mashed potatoes. I'd have to drop everything I was doing and run to the store. Just like today.

Why, I wanted to ask her, *does your suffering have to interfere so much with my life? Why can't I talk to you about some of the things that are bugging me so much these days? Why is it always about YOU?* But these days mouthing off didn't even make her flinch, she was in such a sad headspace.

My life was in need of a major overhaul too. But I had no idea how I could possibly change it. There's not much you can do if you suck at math. I could study harder, maybe, but that had never worked for me in the past. And how do you "get the guy" when there's so much competition out there? It was the same thing with that coveted role in the play, the one I was going to audition for. I knew I didn't stand a chance.

The clouds were low now and purple as a bruise. Shivering, I began to run toward the main street. As the slushy rain spattered my face, curse words spilled from my lips for forgetting my umbrella. I stopped on the corner and waited for a break in traffic before stepping off the curb. For an instant I imagined how guilty my mom would feel if I got struck by a car while I was on an errand for one of her dumb cravings.

When I reached the plaza a few minutes later, I spotted it right away, stuffed into a trash can outside the supermarket doors. Thinking back, maybe I should have just run right past it.

I stopped to check it out. It was an umbrella in gorgeous rainbow shades, like stained glass or a kaleidoscope. Someone had left it there in the can. *Broken,* I thought. I spun a glance around to see if anyone was watching, then yanked it out by the curved handle and snapped it open.

It was perfect. I closed it, tucked it under my arm and hurried into the store. When I stepped out a few minutes later, it was as

The clouds were low now and purple as a bruise. Shivering, I began to run toward the main street. As the slushy rain spattered my face, curse words spilled from my lips for forgetting my umbrella. I stopped on the corner and waited for a break in traffic before stepping off the curb. For an instant I imagined how guilty my mom would feel if I got struck by a car while I was on an errand for one of her dumb cravings.

When I reached the plaza a few minutes later, I spotted it right away, stuffed into a trash can outside the supermarket doors. Thinking back, maybe I should have just run right past it.

I stopped to check it out. It was an umbrella in gorgeous rainbow shades, like stained glass or a kaleidoscope. Someone had left it there in the can. *Broken,* I thought. I spun a glance around to see if anyone was watching, then yanked it out by the curved handle and snapped it open.

It was perfect. I closed it, tucked it under my arm and hurried into the store. When I stepped out a few minutes later, it was as sighing. Oh, and asking me to run to the store to pick up random stuff that she had a craving for. Sometimes it was weird, like a jar of pickled herring, or a box of instant mashed potatoes. I'd have to drop everything I was doing and run to the store. Just like today.

Why, I wanted to ask her, *does your suffering have to interfere so much with my life? Why can't I talk to you about some of the things that are bugging me so much these days? Why is it always about YOU?* But these days mouthing off didn't even make her flinch, she was in such a sad headspace.

My life was in need of a major overhaul too. But I had no idea how I could possibly change it. There's not much you can do if you suck at math. I could study harder, maybe, but that had never worked for me in the past. And how do you "get the guy" when there's so much competition out there? It was the same thing with that coveted role in the play, the one I was going to audition for. I knew I didn't stand a chance.